Jörg Mü

When Dad's Hair Took Off

Translated by Melody Shaw

GECKO PRESS

Dad's hair was sick of being
brushed and combed. It was tired
of hanging around on his head.
It wanted a life of its own.
It wanted to see the world.

One day, it coiled itself, and sprang.

Horrors!

Dad sprang after it.

He flailed his arms about,
shooing it around
the bathroom.

He scolded. He threatened.

He begged
and pleaded.

"Stop!" he shouted. "Stop right there!"
But his hair didn't stop.
It didn't listen. It didn't stay.
It fluttered around him, just out of reach.

Dad lost his temper.

He grabbed a towel and swung,

whirled and whipped it about.

He almost caught his hair, too.

I'm guessing he toppled off the stool

and tangled with the toilet paper.

Whumped into the washing machine–maybe.

Or perhaps the toilet brush tripped him up.

I don't know the details.

He doesn't like to talk about it.

Anyway, he stumbled and fell with a bang

into the bathtub.

My mother poked her head around the door

to see what the hullabaloo was about.

The hair took its chance.

It cut along the hall to the living room,
over the kitchen table, and out through
the open window to freedom.

Before I could say, "Hairsta la vista, baby!"
it was gone.

My father doesn't give up easily.

He grabbed the nearest coat, threw on
some socks and shoes, muttered, "Back
soon!" and was off.

As Dad stepped out the door,
he thought he could see his hair in the
garden, playing on the lawn.
Right under his nose.

Dad crept closer, like a stalking lion
(without its mane).

Slowly and carefully.
Very carefully.

Hiding in the shadows,
staying downwind.

Silent and stealthy.

He crouched low

and leapt!

Nothing there but grass.

For a while, Dad just lay there,
stretched out on the lawn.

Then he picked himself up, dusted
himself off, gave a mighty snort,
and stomped into the basement.

We heard him rootling around.

He came out with a net and a small pot
of wallpaper paste.
We'd bought the net on a family trip,
for catching butterflies. Or fish.
I've no idea what Dad planned to do
with the paste, even though he's told
me the hair story a thousand times.

Then off Dad went, just like that!

Yes, his hair had gone—over the
hills and far away.
But it had left a trail that led
into town.

Dad was very attached to his hair.

Or rather, he *had been.*

Now it was gone, he missed it terribly.

I mean, it had been with Dad
since he was a baby.

They'd done everything together!

His hair had gone to kindergarten with
him, and had been with him through all
his years in school.

It had learned reading, writing and
arithmetic with him.

Together they'd climbed trees,
learned to swim and ride a bike.

They even went to their first sleepover
together.

If Dad was ever at his wits' end,
the hair was there for him to tug.
If he was scared, it stood on end.
It went to the dentist with him.
He took it to the barber.

They hadn't been parted for a single
day, a single minute. Not even when
Dad went to the bathroom.

I mean, hair doesn't just uproot itself.
Everyone knows that.

Dad caught up

with his hair outside a restaurant.
They were serving soup of the day.
And hair is madly attracted to soup,
apparently.

His hair whisked into the restaurant,
and followed the smell at a clip into the
kitchen. It shimmied over to the soup pot.
But the chef noticed.

He slammed the lid

Bang!

onto the pot, shooed the hair out of his
kitchen, and chased it to and fro across
the restaurant.

They met outside:
The hair. The chef. My father.

The chef
hurled his →
spoon in fury.

The hair reacted super quick and swept over the top.

The net brushed by, a hair's breadth away.

The spoon hit my father.

And with that, the hair was off again.

This time, my father was right on its tail.

The hair tried to cut and run at the barber.

It crept into a crypt, ducked into a pond
and lay low in a cellar.

It took a spin around a launderette,
hightailed it into the pet shop,
then showed a clean pair of heels
at the fountain.

It was the perfect game of hide and seek.

But Dad wasn't playing!

He came within a whisker at the department store.

Dad would have
caught his hair for sure

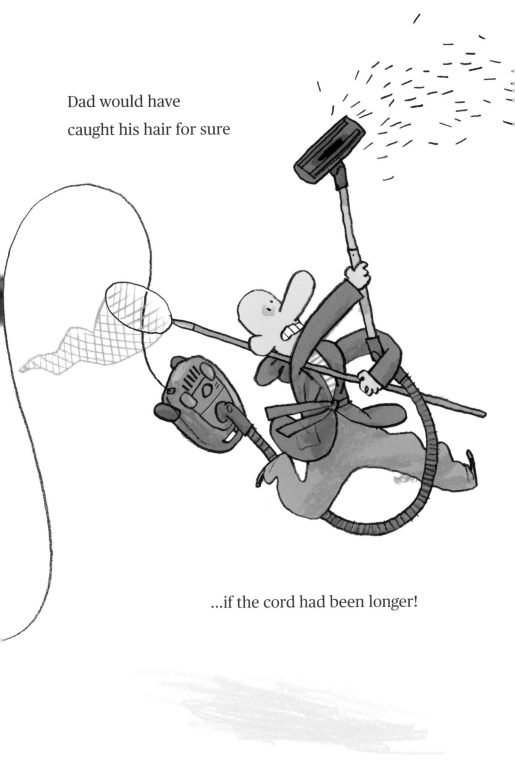

...if the cord had been longer!

The wild hunt continued.

The hair tearing ahead,
my father swearing behind.
You know how it goes.

To cut a long story short:
Dad had to stop at a red light.
His hair had flicked across on the green.
He was a step too late.
He was forced to watch as his hair
slipped into the zoo across the street.

How on earth was he going
to find it here?

Nix at the desert fox.

Zilch at the zebras.

Neither hide nor hair
(of his) in the lion's cage.
(Just as well, is all I can say!)

Nope

And at the hippo, zippo.

The grizzly bear looked suspicious to Dad,
lounging innocently in the sun.
A zookeeper turned up to hose down the
rock and water the shrubs.
The grizzly bear blinked drowsily.
Then a jet of water struck him.

Surprise!

Not so much grizzly
as plain old bear.
The grizzles were Dad's hair.

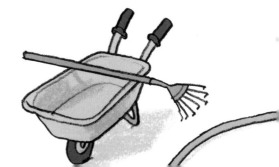

With a gurgle and a gloop in the gutter,
it disappeared down the drain with a
faint burp.

Dad's hair was gone.
There was nothing more
he could do.

The hair hurtled via underground pipes to the sewerage system, through the treatment plant, and into a stream.

town

sewerage system

I learned about this at school.

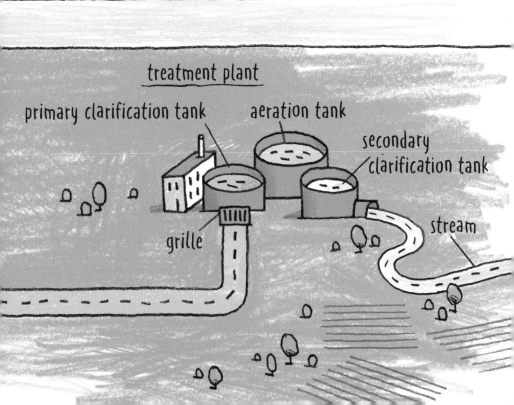

treatment plant

primary clarification tank   aeration tank

secondary
clarification tank

grille

stream

After that, it went with the flow.

From a stream, to a river, to a bigger river,

until at last it reached the sea,

where all rivers flow eventually.

stream

river

Once you've reached the sea, you can travel anywhere in the world.

From that day on,

Dad was bald. His beard still grew.
And all the other hair that nobody needs–
in his ears and nose, for example.

As for the other hair–his proper hair, his
former crowning glory–it wrote to him.
It sent postcards, selfies, and greetings
from abroad.

From *Manhairtan Island*
and the *Sahaira Desert.*
From *Hairizona,*
from the *Antarctic Arc-hairpelago,*
from *Mount Hairverest, Bulghairia*
and *Buenos Haires.*

From hair, there and everywhere...
My father was not amused.

It went on like that for a while.

Then one day, something unbelievable
happened.

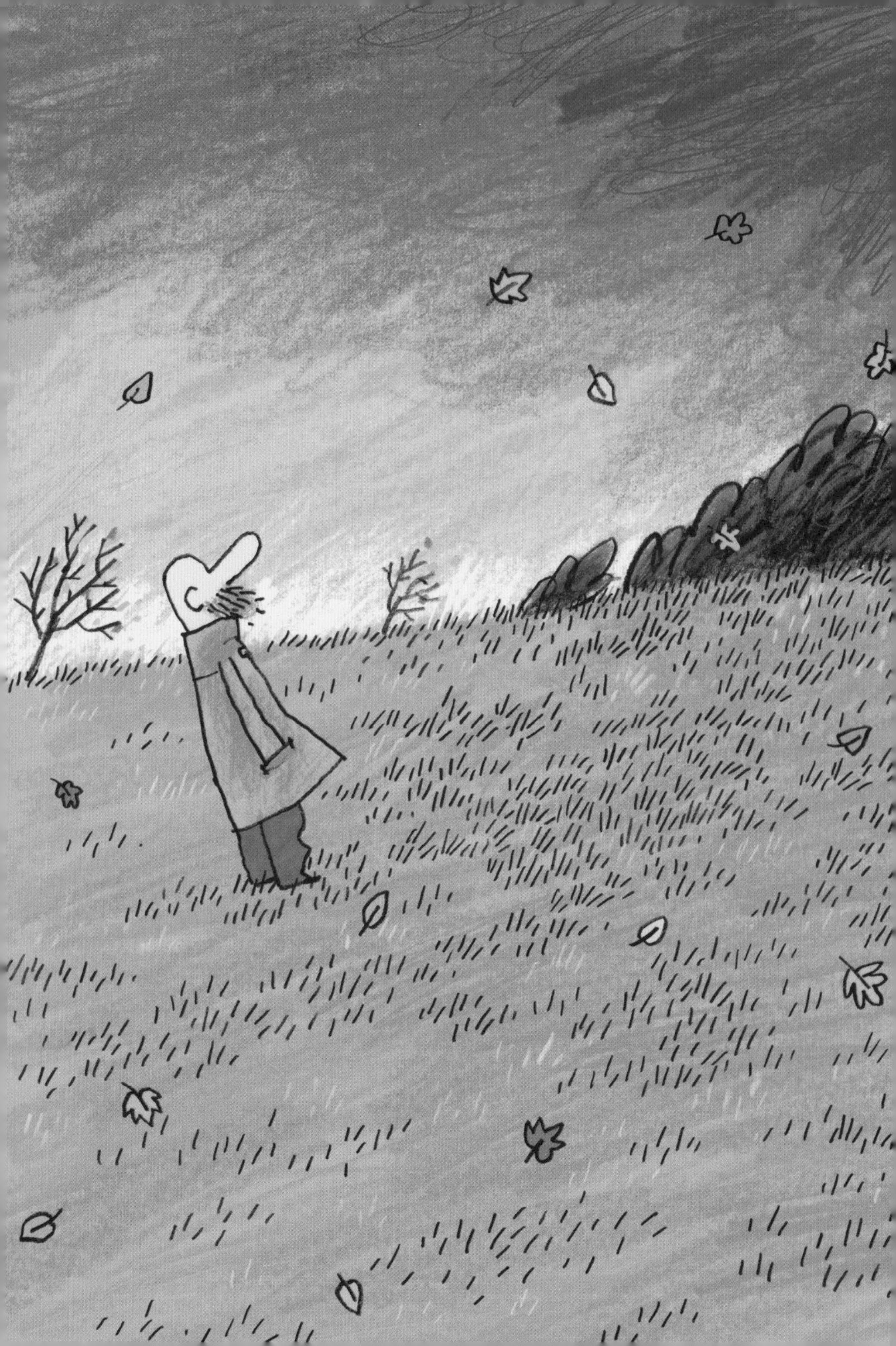

The leaves were falling from the trees.
Dad insisted on going for a walk, so we all
had to go along. The weather wasn't great–
wind, dull sky, dark clouds. My mother and
I hurried back to the warm house. But Dad
stayed outside–he liked gloomy weather.

He stood and stared into the sky as if he
was looking for something. We called him,
but he didn't respond. He just stood there.

It was growing darker and darker.
The sky was closing in on him.
All of a sudden, it began to bucket down.

But not with rain.

With hair.

Dad's hair was back!

And it had so much to tell him.

Jörg Mühle

Jörg Mühle lives in Frankfurt am Main, where he writes and illustrates children's books.

Jörg is best known for his bestselling *Tickle My Ears* board books for babies, and he wrote the picture book *Two for Me, One for You*. He has illustrated many chapter books including *Duck's Backyard* by Ulrich Hub.

Jörg studied at the Offenbach School of Design and the École Nationale Supérieure des Arts Décoratifs in Paris.

This edition first published in 2023 by Gecko Press
PO Box 9335, Wellington 6141, Aotearoa New Zealand
office@geckopress.com

English-language edition © Gecko Press Ltd 2023
Translation © Melody Shaw 2023

Text and illustrations: Jörg Mühle
Title of original edition: *Als Papas Haare Ferien machten*
© 2022 Moritz Verlag, Frankfurt am Main
English-language edition arranged through mundt agency, Düsseldorf

Gecko Press is committed to sustainable practice. We publish books
to be read over and over. We use sewn bindings and high-quality
production and print all our new books using vegetable-based inks
on FSC-certified paper from sustainably managed forests.

The translation of this book was supported by a grant from
the Goethe-Institut

Original language: German
Edited by Penelope Todd
Cover design by Vida Kelly
Printed in China by Everbest Printing Co. Ltd,
an accredited ISO 14001 & FSC-certified printer

ISBN hardback: 9781776575206
ISBN paperback: 9781776575213
Ebook available

For more curiously good books, visit geckopress.com

Gecko Press is a small-by-choice, independent publisher of children's books in translation. We publish a curated list of books from the best writers and illustrators in the world.

Gecko Press books celebrate unsameness. They encourage us to be thoughtful and inquisitive, and offer different—sometimes challenging, often funny—ways of seeing the world. They are printed on high-quality, sustainably sourced paper with stitched bindings so they can be read and re-read.

For more Gecko Press illustrated chapter books, visit our website or your local bookstore. You might like ...

Bruno by Catharina Valckx and Nicolas Hubesch, in which Bruno the cat tells about six of the more interesting days in his life so far.

Yours Sincerely, Giraffe by Megumi Iwasa and Jun Takabatake: letters across the world between a penguin and a giraffe, who try to imagine what the other might look like—all neck or no neck?

Free Kid to Good Home by Hiroshi Ito, a comic for anyone with a potato-faced baby brother who thinks it could be fun to run away (not far) from home.

A Bear Named Bjorn by Delphine Perret for readers who enjoy a gentle bushwalk with an observant bear.

My Happy Life by Rose Lagercrantz and Eva Eriksson, a book about best friends and life in the world of Dani, who has a special ability to be happy and make those around her happy too.

The Yark by Bertrand Santini and Laurent Gapaillard, for readers who enjoy fairy tales and aren't afraid of the crunch of bones in a monster's teeth...

Detective Gordon: The First Case by Ulf Nilsson and Gitte Spee, for detective stories set in a friendly forest, where Detective Gordon seeks justice for all and always makes time for delicious cakes.

Stories of the Night by Kitty Crowther—a magical pink storybook, in which mama bear tells three goodnight stories and the night guardian finally finds someone to tell her it's time for bed.

The Runaways by Ulf Stark and Kitty Crowther, a story about Ulf, whose grandfather hates being in hospital—so together they make a plan to break him out.